The Le of The Giant's Ring

CORA CALAHOUN

Thanks to Katherine for all her
assistance with the illustrations.

For those that visit The Giant's Ring at just the right time of day with just the right amount of light and just the right amount of dark then if you are lucky you will meet The Roshini.

The Roshini live at The Giant's Ring which is to be found on the road to Ballynaratty near Shaws Bridge on the outskirts of Belfast City in The North of Ireland.

If you are lucky and chance upon that right moment then you will, as a little girl called Kiara did one beautiful December day, meet the wonderful Roshini and it will change your life forever.

The Giant's Ring,
Ballynahatty, Shaw's
Bridge, Belfast.

It was very early on a chilly Saturday December morning that Kiara went with her Dad Calum to walk their bouncy little dog called Rascal, an adorable black and white border collie who loved an early morning walk around The Giant's Ring. Her Dad always said that it was a nice quiet wee spot for a walk.

Kiara and her Dad always went early when her Dad was working on Saturdays, which he always did in December as the garden centre where he worked was very busy with Christmas shoppers buying Christmas trees and decorations.

Her distinctively red haired Dad would spend the rest of his day lugging Christmas trees into shopper's cars at the Garden Centre.

They had been at The Giant's Ring many times before and there was nothing to suggest that this day would be any different.

It was bitterly ice cold and the winds from the Irish Sea were howling fiercely. Kiara's straight shoulder length dark black hair blew wildly in the wind as she ran along the top of the banks around the ring with Rascal.

An elastic band to tie it back might have been a good idea but Kiara had little time to find one as they rushed to ensure Rascal got his walk before Dad had to leave for work.

It was barely dawn but Kiara had never felt more alive as she felt the power of the wind against her bare face. Kiara watched some seagulls as they headed toward the trees. It was unusual to see a seagull here so she watched attentively as they flew towards one of the large trees at the edge of the ring.

Her eyes took in the wonder of the beautiful landscape all around her. All of the Belfast Mountains were visible from her vantage point high on top of the bank.

Divis Mountain, Black Mountain and Cave Hill all stood grey and stark against the horizon.

Even though only a few miles from the busy streets of Belfast it was a world apart.

In that moment Kiara felt as if time floated away from her and she stood at the beginning of time. It was just her, the wind, the stones and the distant mountains.

Her Granny Anne would call this a fierce day and
Kiara felt ice cold and so headed instinctively
towards the stones in the middle of the ring to get
some shelter.

Kiara settled herself comfortably against one of the
giant stones to shelter from the mid-winter wind.
She sat sheltered holding her hands against the
ancient stones, watching the seagulls as the sun
rose around The Giants Ring entranced by the
beauty of this magical place.

Then these beautiful rainbow beings appeared from the ground slowly, magically and with grace. They filled the beautiful silence of the dawn with a serene magic that held Kiara in a complete trance. Her dad seemed completely unaware of them and continued to play energetically with Rascal.

The bright glow from the beautiful rainbow creatures lit up the entirety of the ring and filled it with a magical energy.

Pure beams of rainbow-coloured light danced all around The Giants Ring. They changed shape rhythmically and there was no discernible pattern but somehow a magical spiral dance of waterfalls and spinning globes was created which were all dancing in perfect rhythm.

Above all Kiara could feel pure love spreading out from the rainbows. She could feel the energy flowing through her body like a symphony. In the deepest cells of her body. She felt each note as a pulse of rainbow energy surging through every cell in her small seven year old body.

Instinctively she felt drawn towards one particular beam of light. It lit up brightly and twirled around rhythmically captivating her with its beautiful dance. Kiara heard no actual words but could feel the welcome from this particular rainbow being which was shaped like a seagull. She walked slowly across The Giants Ring towards the seagull. The beautiful spiraling dance of rainbows billowed gently around her. She knew that these were The Roshini.

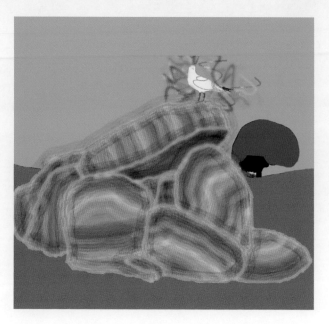

Kiara followed the seagull, entranced and watched as it flew towards the stones at the centre of The Giant's Ring. It landed and perched on top of the highest stone. It swirled and sparkled with a beauty beyond anything Kiara had seen in her seven years of life.

The other rainbow beams of light danced rhythmically towards the standing stones. As more and more beautiful rainbow creatures moved into the stones, they began to glow and pulse with all the beautiful colours of the rainbow. Finally only the seagull remained as the procession of Roshini completed their journey into the stones.

Without words Kiara could feel the rainbow seagull asking her if she wanted to join them in the stones. Kiara walked towards the magical glowing stones and asked what was inside it.

"It is the gateway to the magic land of your dreams," replied the seagull silently.

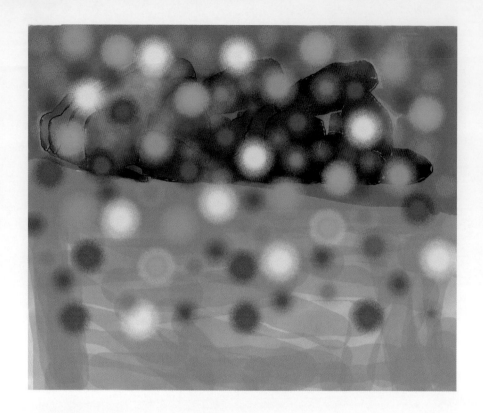

Kiara walked decidedly into the standing stones
following The Roshini. The ground within the
stones opened up and there was a huge warm
cavern with crystal ground bathed in a beautiful
rainbow light radiating from The Roshini who lived
here.

Kiara took off her heavy boots and winter coat and
sat down on the crystal ground amongst The
Roshini.

She felt the warmth of the crystal on her bare feet and touched it with her fingers.

Kiara became aware of a large archway at the edge
of the cavern and as Kiara looked out it she could
see a huge forest full of rainbow trees and birds
which stretched as far as Kiara could see. There
were apple trees, pear trees, kiwi trees, orange
trees, banana trees and many other types of fruit
which Kiara had never seen. A fragrant smell of
fruit and flowers filled the air.

Kiara looked around in amazement at this beautiful forest. She walked on through the forest. She could feel the energy of it as she passed through the trees. She could sense the life force all around her in the majestic tall tree trunks, and in the beautiful red trumpet-like flowers.

All around her flowers of every colour and size created a huge expanse of beauty which stretched as far as Kiara could see. Kiara spotted a small orange butterfly which flitted from one plant to another enjoying the fertile bounty of this wonderful landscape. Kiara followed it deeper into the forest through the undergrowth.

Her little legs grew tired from her wanderings and she sat down on an inviting fallen log which made a perfect seat for her. Kiara rested on the comfortable log enjoying the beautiful view.

Then a bright little rabbit came up to her and began to nibble on a blade of grass right beside her. The whiteness of the rabbit's fur shone brightly in the forest, and even its tiny perfect paws were pure white. The small rabbit jumped up onto the log and cuddled up beside her and fell soundly asleep.

Kiara could feel each breath of the rabbit as she watched it sleep. Kiara felt such a sense of connection to this rabbit and this forest.

She could feel the forest as she breathed, she felt connected to the trees, flowers, grasses, birds, squirrels and rabbits. Her heart beat in unison with the forest as she sat there in silent harmony with the rabbit and forest.

How long this lasted she did not know but after a while, the rabbit stretched wide awake and looked up directly at her with intent.

The rabbit turned slowly, following a glint of light which was flashing through the trees.

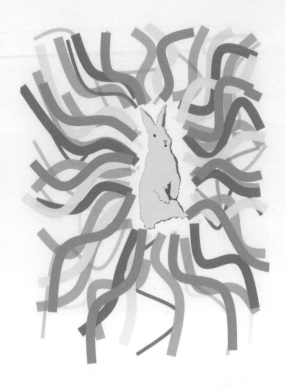

Kiara watched dreamily as it bounded through the trees. Suddenly it stopped and looked back at her, as if to say "what is keeping you? come on, slow coach!" The little furry bundle bobbed impatiently as it waited for Kiara to catch up.

Then they continued together through the forest. Kiara followed as the rabbit weaved its way through the forest, slowly stopping every few minutes to allow Kiara to catch up. Kiara was still in awe from the blaze of colour and smells which enveloped her completely as she walked through the forest.

A blaze of reds, greens, purples, yellows and oranges was suddenly interrupted by the wonder of a clear sparkling huge expanse of water. The rabbit stopped and drank thirstily from the water and then settled down again for another snooze.

Kiara however was drawn to the beautiful water. Quickly she fully immersed herself in the tranquil waters. She floated in the rainbow waves, enjoying the wonder of the amazing colours.

Kiara moved through the water with effortless ease. It was warm with gentle waves which seemed to move her quickly in whichever direction she desired. She floated and splashed in the waters for many hours.

Then as she became tired she floated onto a beautiful sandy beach, surrounded by gorgeous palm trees. The palm tree fruits were about twice the size of a mango, but as Kiara bit into one, she found a delicious sweet-tasting bright green flesh much like a ripe pear. However, it tasted unlike anything Kiara had ever tasted before.

With her tummy full and exhausted from the refreshing swim, Kiara fell into a deep sleep. It was a deep, restful, dreamless sleep and when Kiara woke she found herself back in the cavern where she had arrived.

Kiara knew that it was time to return home. Kiara put on her heavy winter snow boots and with purpose in her step headed back into The Giants Ring.

Life would never be quite the same again. Kiara walked towards Rascal overflowing with energy as she now held the magic of the Roshini within her.